Editor: Anne Ewart   Designer: Martin Shubrook

© Disney Enterprises, Inc./Pixar Animation Studios.
Published in Great Britain in 2002 by Egmont Books Limited, 239 Kensington
High Street, London, W8 6SA. Printed in Italy. ISBN 07498 5635 1

MONSTERS, INC.

CONTENTS

ᗪᎥ𝓈𝓃ℰᎩ·PIXAR
MONSTERS, INC.

Welcome to Monsters, Inc., the largest scream collection and refinery corporation in Monstropolis. We are delighted to have you as part of our team.

Here at Monsters, Inc. we are fully committed to overcoming the current energy crisis, so please practise being scary whenever you can. The more human screams you can collect, the more power we can generate for Monstropolis.

I wish you every success within the Company.

Yours sincerely,

Henry J. Waternoose

MONSTERS, INC.

JAMES P. SULLIVAN

0069-0421-2000
SCARER
SCARE FLOOR F

MONSTERS, INC.

MIKE WAZOWSKI

0061-0210-2000
SCARE ASSISTANT
SCARE FLOOR F

Please fill in the security card before entering the premises.

(YOUR NAME)

0068-0871-2002

SCARER TRAINEE
SCARE FLOOR F

(YOUR PICTURE)

MEET THE TEAM AT
ONSTERS, INC.

2.5 metres

2 metres

1.5 metres

1 metre

0.5 metres

SULLEY

Meet James P. Sullivan, Monsters, Inc.'s Top Scarer! Known as Sulley to his friends, you can learn a lot from this most professional of monsters!

ROZ

Roz controls the paperwork at Monsters, Inc. She makes sure the Scarers are given the right children to scare every time. It is advisable to stay on her good side!

MIKE

No one loves the business of scaring more than Mike Wazowski. As Sulley's scare assistant, Mike makes sure he keeps the furry fellow in top scaring shape.

CELIA

Celia Mae, the receptionist at Monsters, Inc., is the public face of the company and your first point of contact. She will do her best to help you with any questions you may have.

MR. WATERNOOSE

Henry J. Waternoose is the third generation of Waternooses to run Monsters, Inc. He has transformed it into the modern energy giant that it is today, and would do absolutely anything to keep his company afloat.

RANDALL

Randall Boggs has the ability to blend into any background, like a chameleon. It has made him one of the most successful Scarers at Monsters, Inc. But watch out for his competitive side.

DISNEY · PIXAR
MONSTERS, INC.

It was a typical morning in Monstropolis and Sulley and Mike were heading off to work. "What are you doing?" asked Mike, as Sulley dragged him away from his car. "Mikey, there's a scream shortage. We're walking!" replied Sulley.

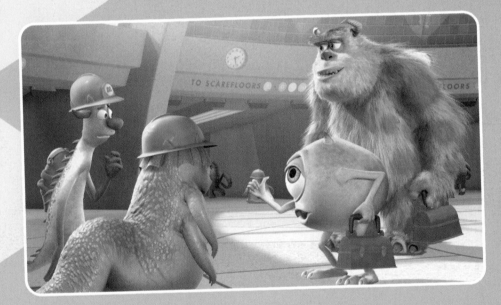

Soon, Sulley and Mike arrived at Monsters, Inc. "Good luck, Mr Sullivan," called Needleman, a skinny, yellow monster who was a big fan of Sulley's. "Hey, you're making him lose his focus," said Mike. "Uh, sorry!" replied Smitty, Needleman's friend.

Mike went to see his girlfriend, Celia. "Happy birthday, Schmoopsie Poo! Tonight I'm going to take you to Harryhausen's," said Mike, smoothly. "Oh, Mike! It's impossible to get a reservation there!" replied Celia, excitedly.

In the locker room, Sulley and Mike prepared for their day. "You know, pal, she's the one!" said Mike. He opened his locker and put in his contact lens. "I'm happy for you," said Sulley, as he polished his horns.

Suddenly, Mike's locker door slammed shut and Randall appeared. "What do ya know! It scares little kids *and* little monsters!" smirked Randall. "Uh, I wasn't scared. I have...allergies," stammered Mike.

"What a creep! One of these days I'm going to let *you* teach that guy a lesson!" Mike told Sulley, as soon as Randall was out of earshot. "Assistants, please report to your stations," announced the tannoy. It was time for work to begin.

All across the Scare Floor, scare assistants prepared scream canisters and called down doors ready for the Scarers to start work. The blinds were lowered and everyone waited for the action to begin!

"We've got Scarers coming out!" called the Floor Manager. A silence swept the Scare Floor. The assistants watched in awe as the Scarers, lead by Sulley, emerged from the shadows and lined up opposite their doors.

"...Three, two, one, scream!" cried the Floor Manager. Sulley entered his first room and the scream canisters started to fill. "I'm feeling good today, Mikey!" said Sulley. "That a boy! Another door comin' right up!" said Mike.

Randall's scare assistant, Fungus, checked the Scare Floor score-board. "You're still behind, Randall," said Fungus. "Grrrr! Just get me another door!" snarled Randall. He didn't want to spend one more day being second best to Sulley.

Suddenly, at the door station next to Sulley's and Mike's, a scare assistant spotted a sock on his Scarer's back. "Twenty-three nineteen! We have a twenty-three nineteen!" cried the scare assistant in panic.

"Red Alert! George Sanderson, please remain motionless! Prepare for decontamination!" blasted the tannoy. "Get it off!" yelled George, as the CDA (Child Detection Agency) rushed to the scene.

In seconds, the CDA agents removed the toxic sock with tongs and pulled a curtain around George. Fur flew as the decontamination process began. "Take a break everyone. We gotta reset the system," said the Floor Manager.

At the end of their busy shift, Mike and Sulley walked down the corridor. "Another day like this and that scare record's in the bag," said Sulley. "That's right, baby! And what a night of romance I've got ahead of me!" added Mike.

"Hello, Wazowski. Fun-filled evening planned? And I'm sure you filed your paperwork correctly," croaked Roz. "Oh, no! My scare reports!" cried Mike. He was just about to run back to fetch his paperwork when Celia appeared at his side.

"Hey, Googly Bear! Want to get going?" asked Celia. "Uh…it's just…" stammered Mike. "…It's just that I forgot about some paperwork I was supposed to file. Mike was reminding me," interrupted Sulley.

Sulley was more than happy to help his old friend out. He set off, back to the Scare Floor, trying to remember Mike's instructions. But while he was sorting out Mike's files, Sulley noticed a single door, still in its station.

The red light above the door shone brightly, which meant that the door was active and lead directly to a child's bedroom. Sulley was confused. Why would an active door be left out on the Scare Floor with no one around? He put down Mike's paperwork and walked towards it.

Continued on page 16…

THE SCARE FLOOR

The Scare Floor is the heart of Monsters, Inc. It is where the monster world connects with the bedroom of every human child via a computerised delivery system. The most talented monsters in the business work here, collecting human screams ready for refining and distribution.

REMEMBER!! Kids are toxic!! You must have no contact with them at any time!

PICK A CARD

The scare assistants use coded CARDKEYs – one for each child – to tell the system which door to call down.

Work out the sums to find out which CARDKEY belongs to which door.

3x3/6+4/7x7

16-4/2x2/7x3

64/36/7

6/14/45

12/4/21

8x8/6x6/4+3

14-8/2x7/9x5

9/10/49

LEARN THE ROUTINE

It is important to have a thorough understanding of how the Scare Floor works.

Can you put these procedures into the correct order?

- [ ] THE SCARE ASSISTANT CALLS UP A DOOR FROM THE VAULT
- [ ] THE SCARER GOES THROUGH THE DOOR INTO THE CHILD'S BEDROOM
- [ ] THE DOOR ARRIVES AND IS CONNECTED TO THE DOOR STATION
- [ ] THE CHILD'S SCREAMS ARE COLLECTED IN THE CANISTERS
- [ ] A RED LIGHT GOES ON ABOVE THE DOOR TO SHOW THAT IT IS READY
- [ ] THE SCARER SCARES THE CHILD

SCREAM CONTROL

The scream canisters are always handled with care. The smallest leak could cause an uncontrollable power surge which could result in disaster.

Check the level of each canister against its number to find out how many are leaking.

THE SCORE-BOARD

At one end of the Scare Floor is a huge screen. It shows the scare totals for each of the Scarers as well as the total number of children scared. The Scarer with the highest total becomes the Scarer of the Month. This is a very impressive award to win and has been held by James P. Sullivan for the last year.

WHICH SCARER?

Read the score-board to find out who...

Is below Ranft?
Has the number 1 at the end of his score?
Has a higher score than Pauley?
Has five letters in his name?

CHILDREN SCARED

SCARE FLOOR F	SCARE TOTALS	
SULLIVAN	99,479	
RANDALL	99,351	
RANFT	79,012	
LUCKEY	68,245	
RIVERA	67,992	
PETERSON	67,236	
JONES	66,101	
SANDERSON	58,986	
PLESUSKI	55,735	
SCHMIDT	44,421	
PAULEY	41,918	
WARD	38,620	
GERSON	12,431	

WELL DONE, SULLEY

As Scarer of the Month, James P. Sullivan's pictures are displayed on the wall.

Which two pictures look exactly the same?

SCREAM TOTAL

Much of the excitement on the Scare Floor comes from the changing totals of Monsters, Inc.'s top Scarers, James P. Sullivan and Randall Boggs.

Complete the totals to find out who has collected the most screams after Door 4.

Door 1

SCARE	TOTALS
8	8
7	7

Door 2

SCARE	TOTALS
6	14
9	16

Door 3

SCARE	TOTALS
11	
10	

Door 4

SCARE	TOTALS
10	
8	

15

...Continued from page 11

"Huh? Hello? There's a door here," Sulley called out. The Scare Floor remained silent. Gingerly, Sulley opened the door and peered into the child's room on the other side. "Pssst! Is anybody scaring in here?" asked Sulley.

Sulley could see that the room was empty. He was just about to close the door and return to Mike's filing when...

thump!

he heard a noise behind him. Sulley turned around to see...

"Ahhhhhhhh!"

a little girl holding on to his tail!

Quickly, Sulley grabbed a pair of tongs and picked the little girl up. Sulley knew that contact with a human child was extremely dangerous and could even prove to be fatal. He needed to put her back into her room, and fast!

Sulley reached over and opened the door. He leaned in and dropped the little girl back into her room. But as Sulley shut the door, the little girl ran through his legs and back on to the Scare Floor.

17

Sulley was beginning to panic. He grabbed the little girl and carried her all the way into her bedroom and put her down on her bed. Now he had enough time to escape back on to the Scare Floor, without her following him.

But on his way out, Sulley knocked into a wardrobe and became tangled up in the little girl's mobile. Things were going from bad to worse. Ouside the little girl's room, Sulley froze, as he heard a noise.

Someone was coming! Sulley sprinted across the Scare Floor and down the corridor into the locker room. Frantically, Sulley looked around for somewhere to hide all the toxic items he was carrying.

"Whew!" sighed Sulley, as he managed to stuff all the child's things into one locker. Now he could go home and try to forget about everything that had happened. But as Sulley walked out of the locker room...

..."Ahhhhhhhh!"
He saw the little girl clinging on to his back. "Kitty!" she called, as she dropped down to the floor. Sulley backed into the lockers – he was trapped! The dangerous child was surrounding every exit.

Frantically, Sulley looked around for something to help him. He spotted an empty bag on top of the lockers. He pulled it down and carefully scooped the little girl up and into the bag.

Sulley ran with the bag back to the Scare Floor. He breathed a sigh of relief when he saw the door, still in place. This was going to work out fine, after all. He ran up to the door and was just about to open it when…

…he heard the doorknob rattle. Someone was coming out from inside the bedroom! Sulley stopped, frozen with fright. He ducked down behind the door station and crouched in fear as the door opened.

An angry Randall came out of the room and ejected the door. Now that the door was gone, there was no way Sulley could put the child back into her room without the correct door cardkey. Sulley needed help!

At Harryhausen's, Mike and Celia were enjoying their romantic meal. "Someone asked me who I thought was the most beautiful monster in all of Monstropolis. And do you know who I said?" asked Mike. Celia waited for Mike's answer with a smile.

"...Sulley?" said Mike, as Sulley's panicked face suddenly appeared at the restaurant window. "Sulley!!!?" asked a very confused Celia. Mike squirmed with annoyance, as he watched Sulley lumber into the restaurant, with a big, black bag.

"Hi, guys! What a coincidence running into you here!" said Sulley, as he squeezed himself into the seat beside Mike. "Look in the bag!" whispered Sulley to Mike, from behind the menu.

"What bag?" asked Mike. He looked under the table but he couldn't see a bag. Then he spotted it, walking across the restaurant, with little human feet poking out from the bottom!

Sulley spotted it, too. "Uh, they don't have anything I like here. 'Bye, Celia!" cried Sulley. He leapt up from the table and tried to catch the bag before anyone else noticed it.

But by now the little girl was out of the bag and all the monsters in the restaurant had seen her. There was a panic as everyone scrambled for the exits. "There's a kid here! *A human kid!!*" screamed the sushi chef, as he called the CDA.

With lightning speed, Mike scooped the little girl into one of the restaurant's take-out boxes. "Come on!" shouted Sulley, as he grabbed the box and ran out of the restaurant.

In seconds, the CDA arrived with helicopters and tanks. "We have an eight-three-five in progress. Stand clear, please!" blared the loud speakers. The CDA agents abseiled down into the danger zone.

The CDA collected all the monsters from the restaurant together for decontamination, including Celia. Sulley and Mike watched from an alley in shock. "Well, I don't think that date could have gone any worse," muttered Mike.

Continued on page 30...

DECONTAMINATION

If you do come into contact with a human child, the first rule is DON'T PANIC. Calmly raise the alarm that there is a 'Twenty-three nineteen' situation at which point the CDA (Child Detection Agency) will be notified.

1	2 abc	3 def
4 ghi	5 jkl	6 mno
7 pqrs	8 tuv	9 wxyz

DIAL H-E-L-P!

Which numbers should you press to dial h-e-l-p?

CHILD SAFETY

It is not just the human child that is dangerous, but their belongings, too, as they could easily contain traces of unstable screams.

Unscramble the letters to find out what was safely destroyed under this detonator dome.

CONTAMINATION CODES

Follow the lines to find out which code should be used for contact with which item.

9-17   **57-12**   **43-12**   **4-13**

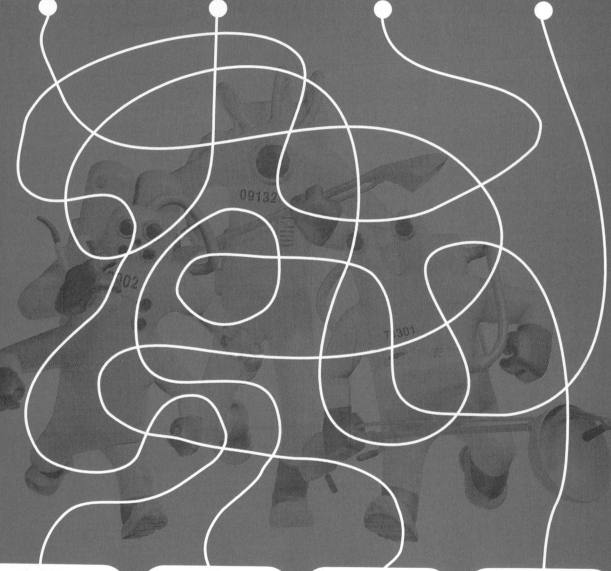

a child's ball

a child's doll

a child's slipper

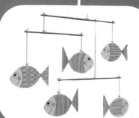

a child's mobile

THE SIMULATOR

Welcome to the simulator room – Monsters, Inc.'s impressive training facility. It is equipped with the latest state-of-the-art technology and is especially designed to ensure that our Scarers reach their full scaring potential.

MS. FLINT'S ABC OF SCARING

Ms. Flint has three helpful hints for you to remember whilst training in the simulator room.

a. Focus on technique. You will be able to develop your own style in time.

b. Study your CDA handbook. Fake CDA emergencies trip up many new recruits.

c. An open cupboard door is a dangerous door! Enter quickly and shut it straight behind you.

THINK SCARY

You can prepare for the simulator room by imagining yourself as one of the top Scarers.

Draw a picture of your favourite Scarer below.

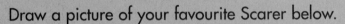

Your monster

PRACTICE MAKES PERFECT

Thaddeus Bile is having a second try in the simulator room.

What are the 10 differences in his second attempt?

①

②

TRAINING GAME

When training in the simulator room it is important to focus on these two techniques.

WATERNOOSE JUMP AND GROWL

This is one of the oldest and most reliable scaring tactics practised at Monsters, Inc. In one quick motion, throw the door open and leap into the child's room, letting out a loud growl.

BOGGS QUICK REVEAL

Perfected by Randall Boggs, a non-chameleon Scarer can also use this technique to the same effect. Silently sneak up to a child's bed and stay perfectly still until the child opens its eyes.

START

Equipment needed: a dice and a counter for each trainee.

Are you ready? Then let the training begin...

Decide which technique you want to practise. Place all the counters at START and take it in turns to roll the dice and move your counter through the simulator room. When you land in the red zone, perform your technique and roll the dice to see how scary you were – 6 points for scream-tastic; 1 point for scream-awful.

Now, return to the safety of the cupboard, avoiding all obstacles in your way. The first monster to reach the cupboard door with a perfect 6 is the winner!

It is always good to watch others as you can often spot mistakes that you wouldn't notice in your own performance. Playing this game with other trainees has proved to be a very effective way of learning.

Leave the cupboard door open! Go back to start

SCARE!!!!

SCARE!!!!

SCARE!!!!

SCARE!!!!

SCARE!!!!

SCARE!!!!

Get caught up in the curtain! Lose 2 points

Touch the child! Lose all your points

Trip on skateboard! Lose 1 point

Become scared by the child! Return to start

...Continued from page 23

Sulley and Mike took the little girl back to their apartment and prepared themselves for the horror that was a small child. "It's all right! As long as it doesn't come near us, we're gonna be OK," said Mike.

But then, the little girl started to cry. The lights in the apartment became incredibly bright and Sulley and Mike could hear the CDA's helicopters whirring outside their window. "Make it stop, Sulley! Make it stop!" cried Mike.

Sulley wasn't sure what to do but by chance Mike tumbled over into the bin. "Hee-hee-hee!" laughed the little girl. This time every single light in the building surged. And then, there was darkness.

"What was *that?*" asked Sulley. "I have no idea, but it would be really great if it didn't do it ever again," murmured Mike. He pulled himself out of the bin and stormed over to his desk.

In the candlelight, Mike tried to come up with a plan. "Hot air balloons…too expensive. Giant slingshot…too conspicuous. Enormous wooden horse…too Greek," said Mike.

The little girl had fun drawing lots of pictures, but before long she started to yawn.
"Uh, Mike, I think she's getting tired," said Sulley.
"Well then, why don't you find some place for it to sleep while I think of a plan?" replied Mike.

Sulley picked up a cereal packet and poured a trail of cereal into his bedroom. "OK, I'm making a nice place...hey, that's *my* bed!" said Sulley, when he turned around and saw the little girl climbing into his bed.

She held up one of her drawings. "That looks like Randall. Is he your monster?" asked Sulley. The little girl nodded. Sulley opened his cupboard door to show her that it was empty. "See? No monster in here," he said.

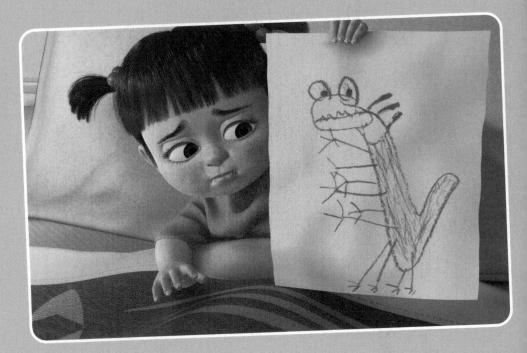

As Sulley watched the little girl sleeping, he began to feel quite attached to her. Sulley decided that whatever Mike's plans were, he would find a way to take the little girl back into Monsters, Inc. and find her door.

The next morning, Sulley and Mike walked up to Monsters, Inc. carrying the little girl in disguise. "This is crazy. Just think about a few names, will you? Loch Ness, the Abominable Snowman. They've all got one thing in common, pal. Banishment!" ranted Mike.

When the doors of Monsters, Inc. opened, Sulley and Mike saw hundreds of CDA agents, swarming all over the lobby. Returning the little girl to her room was not going to be an easy task.

Suddenly, Sulley and Mike realised that their little monster had wandered off. She was wobbling straight towards Mr. Waternoose and the CDA agents!

Sulley's and Mike's jaws dropped open with shock. "Don't panic," instructed Sulley. "Don't tell me not to panic! This is not OK!" replied Mike. The two friends were dumbstruck.

"Boo!" called the little girl, and she tapped Mr. Waternoose on his leg. "No, not now, not now," shrugged Mr. Waternoose. But then he turned around and saw the little girl standing beside him!

"James! Is this one yours?" asked Mr. Waternoose. "Actually that's my cousin's sister's...uh daughter, Sir," replied Sulley, nervously. "Yeah, it's *Bring an Obscure Relative to Work day*," added Mike.

Sulley and Mike grabbed the little girl and ran out of the lobby and into the locker room. "Wait here, while I get its door cardkey," Mike told Sulley. "But she can't stay here. This is the men's room!" exclaimed Sulley. "It's fine!" said Mike.

"Roz, Randall was working late last night out on the Scare Floor. I really need the cardkey for the door he was using," said Mike. "You didn't hand in your paperwork last night. This office is now closed," croaked Roz.

When Mike returned to the locker room he saw Sulley playing hide-and-seek with the little girl. "What are you doing?" asked Mike. But before Sulley could answer, the little girl started pointing fearfully over his shoulder.

The frightened little girl had spotted Randall, standing outside the locker room. Sulley and Mike grabbed her and ducked into a toilet cubicle, just as Randall entered the room.

Then, Fungus rushed in, holding a newspaper. "The child," he cried, pointing to the front page. "You just get the machine up and running, I'll take care of the kid," replied Randall. "And when I find whoever let it out...they're dead!"

Sulley and Mike gulped and waited for Randall to leave. Then they ran to the Scare Floor with the little girl hidden behind Sulley's back. "We'll just call her door down and send her home. You got her cardkey, right?" asked Sulley. "Of course," lied Mike.

Without Sulley seeing, Mike grabbed a cardkey from a nearby scare assistant and called down its door. "That's not Boo's door!" said Sulley. "Boo? What's Boo?" cried Mike. "That's what I decided to call her," replied Sulley.

"You're not supposed to *name* it! Once you name it, you start getting attached to it! Now put that thing back where it came from," argued Mike, and he opened the door and pointed inside. But Sulley stood firm.

Suddenly, Sulley and Mike realised that the whole Scare Floor was watching them. "We're rehearsing for a play," explained Mike, nervously. Just then, they realised something else. Boo had disappeared!

Continued on page 44...

BETTER HEALTH, BETTER STEALTH

Children are becoming more fearless by the day. It is important to stay in top shape so that you scare to your full potential every time – and if need be, make a swift and agile exit to avoid a security alert.

MONSTER WORKOUT

Practise this workout every morning.

	Monday	Tuesday	Wednesday	Thursday	Friday
crouch down and leap up five times					
open and close a door ten times					
jump over an obstacle five times					
fall to the floor ten times					
stand still for two minutes					

The Monster Workout is ideal as a warm up before going on to the Scare Floor. Please also be sure to follow the basic Repetitive Scare Injury guidelines shown on the right.

Basic RSI Guidelines:

1. Stoop, stand and stretch
2. For every mean face, make a happy face
3. A gargle a day keeps the hoarsies away
4. Clean horns make healthy horns
5. Sing after you scream
6. Avoid unnecessary exposure to kids
7. Know your layout - don't squint in the dark
8. Practise Deep Bellowing exercises
9. Stretch your wings
10. Exercise your eyes - then put them back
11. Flex your tentacles - don't keep them curled
12. Wash your claws after every shift

WELL PRESENTED

Once your health is looked after you need to dress to impress. Well-groomed fur, clean claws and slime-free tentacles are a must.

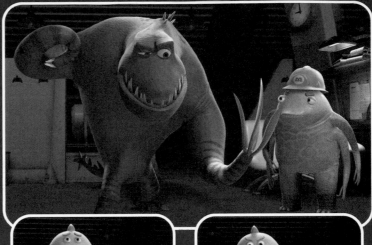

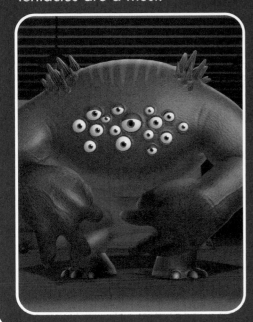

Keep your teeth clean so they glint in the dark. Keep your claws sharpened so they never split. Take care of your eyes – even if you have lots.

GIVE THEM A BRUSH

Follow the code to find out which brand of toothpaste is recommended by Monsters, Inc.

a	b	c	d	e	f	g
z	y	x	w	v	u	t

h	i	j	k	l	m	n
s	r	q	p	o	n	m

o	p	q	r	s	t	u
l	k	j	i	h	g	f

v	w	x	y	z
e	d	c	b	a

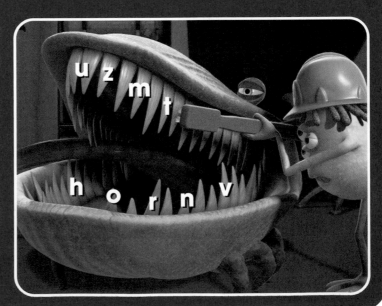

THE NOTICE-BOARD

Please check with Celia Mae on reception if you would like to place a notice here.

CONSERVE SCREAM
Take a walk!

FU...

$59 ⁹⁹⁹

Single Lens
2-D Special

CYCLOPS OPTICAL

HATS
MULTIPLE HEAD SPECIAL
$42 ⁹⁹⁹

REALLY BIG 'N' TALL

COMPANIES
DON'T SCARE
MONSTERS DO.™

BERMUDA
TRIANGLE
GETAWAY

REPLACEMENT

Bring on the Goyles!

AS SEEN ON TV

ORE

AFTE

BOWLING TEAM
TRY-OUTS

Friday at 6:00
(slitherers welcome!)

Monsters, Inc. Scream Team
ASSISTANT OF THE MONTH!

"Hey, just doin' my job!"

MIKE WAZOWSKI

Congratulations Mike! From all of us at:

Monsters, Inc.
We Scare Because We Care

RULE #1

if we don't scare the customer...

somebody else will.™

© 2000 Motivational Scarers Resource

SCREAM POWER

Here at Monsters, Inc., we are dedicated to producing as much refined scream as possible. Shown below are a few ways our refined screams help to power Monstropolis.

Scream-O-Meter

3080051

Power for:

watching TV

vacuuming

reading at night

listening to music

driving to work

Due to the current energy crisis in Monstropolis it is important as an employee of Monsters, Inc. to conserve scream at every opportunity.

Make a list of everything you did today that used scream power.

Make a list of what you could do to conserve scream.

...Continued from page 37

Sulley and Mike were on the look out for Boo. Suddenly, they heard a loud cry. "Michael Wazowski!" screeched Celia. She was still wearing the CDA safety collar from her experience at Harryhausen's, and she was very angry.

"Last night at the sushi restaurant was one of the worst nights of my entire life!" continued Celia. Her snakes were as angry as she was. Mike could see Randall listening to Celia's screeches and he knew he had to do something.

Quickly, Mike grabbed Celia and gave her a big kiss to stop her talking about their disastrous evening. If Randall found out that he and Sulley had been involved with the child they would be in big trouble!

But Celia's outburst had made Randall suspicious. He opened his paper and studied the front cover. "Wazowski! Hmmmm," thought Randall, when he noticed that the child's sighting had been at a sushi bar.

Mike ran away from Celia and Randall as quickly as he could. He needed to find Sulley and Boo and let them know the danger they were in. Mike had just stopped for a minute to catch his breath when…

…Randall appeared beside him. "Where's the kid?" demanded Randall. "Er…" stammered Mike. "At lunch-time the kid's door will be in my station. You'll have half an hour to put the kid back," said Randall.

When Mike found Sulley he told him the good news. "I've got us a way out of this mess. But we've gotta hurry," he said. When they reached the Scare Floor, Mike saw Boo's door in place. "There it is! Just like Randall said!" cried Mike.

"Randall?" asked Sulley. "One-two-three-four, get the kid back through the door!" chanted Mike, in an effort to hurry Sulley up. "Mike, we can't trust Randall! He's after Boo! I don't like this," said Sulley.

"You wanted her door and here it is! Now let's move," said Mike. He couldn't understand why Sulley was hesitating at such an important time. There was no choice, he would just have to prove to Sulley that everything was OK.

"Mike, wait!" cried Sulley. But Mike didn't listen. He ran straight into Boo's room and started jumping on her bed. Sulley watched in horror as a large, yellow box flew up from behind the bed and captured Mike.

Sulley held on to Boo tightly. He dropped down behind a nearby desk and watched the lid to the yellow box being clamped tightly shut.

Before long, Randall emerged from Boo's room, carrying the large, yellow box. He placed it carefully on top of a cart of scream canisters and wheeled it off the Scare Floor.

Sulley and Boo tried to follow Randall but they lost him and came to a dead end. "Where are you, Mike?" called Sulley. Just then, Boo pulled a secret lever and a hidden panel opened to reveal a long, dark corridor.

At the other end of the corridor, Mike was strapped into a strange-looking machine. "Where's the kid?" demanded Randall. "I don't know anything!" replied Mike. Randall smirked and returned to the control panel.

Randall pushed the levers to start the machine but, mysteriously, nothing happened. When Randall went to investigate, Sulley and Boo rushed in and pulled Mike free from the machine.

"We gotta get outta here, now!" cried Mike. "Follow me, I have an idea," said Sulley. He led Mike through the corridors of Monsters, Inc. and into the simulator room. "Mr. Waternoose!" cried Sulley, as he burst into the room.

"The child!" cried Mr. Waternoose. "Randall was trying to kidnap her. He's got a machine for collecting screams that he was gonna test on her!" garbled Mike. "Does anyone else know about this?" asked Mr. Waternoose. "No, Sir," replied Mike.

"Good," said Mr. Waternoose, as he called up a door. "Uh, Sir, that's not her door," said Mike. "I know. It's yours," replied Mr. Waternoose, before pushing Sulley and Mike, with Randall's help, through the door into a snowy wilderness.

Continued on page 54… 49

THE CANTEEN

Take your pick from the wide choice of food available in the Monsters, Inc. canteen. If you would like to try something a little different, the Chef's specials come highly recommended.

TODAY'S LUNCH

Draw a line to link together the names
of the three starters

Snail •   • stings

Toad •   • slime

Bee •   • warts

Pulp Pot Pie
Macaroni & Sleaze
Beak Stroganoff

Invertebrate Medley
Jaundiced Eye Cream
Fresh Mould Cup

CHEF'S SPECIAL

Follow the recipes to make these two monster dishes.

PICKLED EYEBALLS

1. Crack the shells of two cold hardboiled eggs, but leave them on the eggs. Place them in a container with all the other ingredients.

2. Place the container in the fridge for two days. Then take out the eggs and peel off their shells.

Umm, deliciously slimy!

Ingredients
2 hardboiled eggs
1 cup of water
1 cup of vinegar
a teaspoon of salt
10 drops of food colouring

BUG SURPRISE

1. Lay three lengths of fizzy sticks on a plate and place a teacake on top.

2. Place a large sweet next to the teacake for a head and then different sweets for feet and eyes. Hold it all in place with icing.

The legs are particularly crunchy!

Ingredients
3 teacakes
fizzy sticks
icing pens
sweets

PAPERWORK

When you are working in such a large corporation as Monsters, Inc. it is extremely important that the paperwork procedures are followed at all times.

ADVICE FROM ROZ

Paperwork, my friends, is what keeps Monsters, Inc. running. It needs to be completed on time and filed correctly. I'm watching you.

ON TIME

Put these children into order from most recently to least recently scared.

GIBBS, MARY	**17:10**
BROWN, SAM	**18:00**
RAY, IAN	**16:50**
LI, JAY	**17:45**
RICHIE, JILL	**15:35**

IN ORDER

Put these sheets into alphabetical order.

Scare Floor S

MONSTERS, INC.

Scare Floor F

MONSTERS, INC.

Scare Floor B

MONSTERS, INC.

Scare Floor U

MONSTERS, INC.

Scare Floor J

FULLY CORRECTED

Ring each of the five mistakes on the second form.

1

MONSTERS, INC.

FOR OFFICE USE ONLY	
NM#: 50126/00-B	
LO: 09-211#	TB: ROZ

M.I. SCARE REPORT SUBJ: GIBBS, MARY #40046/00-A

AGE: 4	Race: Caucasian	Yeild: 25suv-55suv
GENDER: F	Status: 2	Status: Stage 2

Description:
Energetic, imaginative, artistic, giggler, prone to persistant temper tantrums.

Capacity: 25suv-55suv @16su/cv +/-.6cd pot. cap: 1400

2

MONSTERS, INC.

FOR OFFICE USE ONLY	
NM#: 50126/00-B	
LO: 09-211#	TB:

M.I. SCARE REPORT SUBJ: GIBBS, MARG #40046/00-A

AGE: 44	Race: Caucasian	Yeild: 25suv-55suv
GENDER: M	Status: 2	Status: Stage 2

Description:
Energetic, imaginative, artistic, giggler, prone to persistant temper tantrums.

Capacity: 25suv-55suv @16su/cv +/-.6cd pot. cap: 140

...Continued from page 49

In the snowy wilderness, the Abominable Snowman invited Sulley and Mike back to his cave. But all Sulley could think about was how to return to Monsters, Inc. and save his Boo. "You'll love it here. Wait until you see the local village," said the Abominable Snowman.

"A village? Where is it?" cried Sulley. He knew that if there was a village there would be a child's bedroom with a cupboard door leading back into Monsters, Inc. Sulley made himself a makeshift sleigh and set off straight away.

Meanwhile, back at Monsters, Inc., Randall had strapped Boo into his scream extraction machine. Under the watchful eye of Mr. Waternoose, Randall was putting their evil plan into action.

Sulley's plan worked! He had found a way back into Monsters, Inc.! He ran as fast as he could to the secret corridor. He could hear Boo's screams coming from up ahead.

The Scream Extractor was almost at Boo's face. "Kitty! Kitty! Eeeeeeeeeh!" cried Boo, in terror. "Boo?! Nooooooooo!" roared Sulley, as he burst into the secret room and threw the machine against the wall.

"Kitty!" cried Boo. "I'm sorry, Boo. Let's get out of here!" said Sulley. He gently picked Boo up and held her in his arms. "Stop him! Don't let them get away!" cried Mr. Waternoose.

Randall raced after Sulley and Boo. He used all his sneaky tricks to try to steal Boo back. But just in time, Mike appeared and came to Sulley's rescue. Sulley and Mike ran away with Boo, as fast as they could.

Suddenly, Celia appeared. "Michael, tell me what's going on right now!" she cried. "OK. You know the kid that they're looking for? Sulley let her in and now Randall's trying to kill us," said Mike. Celia was so surprised that she let go.

Sulley and Mike knew that Randall was close behind. But suddenly, they heard Celia's voice on the tannoy. "Attention! Randall Boggs has just broken the all-time scare record!" Randall was trapped by excited monsters, crowding around him.

"There it is!" cried Sulley, when he spotted Boo's door. The three friends grabbed on to a door and rode out of the Scare Floor and into the door vault. "Don't look down!" cried Sulley.

Suddenly, Randall appeared and grabbed Boo. He carried her away on a different track. Boo's screams energised Randall's door and he carried her through into the room on the other side.

Sulley leapt down and tried to climb through the door, but Randall pushed him back. As Sulley clung desperately to the ledge of the door, Randall stamped on his hand.

Boo could see that her Kitty was in trouble. "Roooaarr!" she cried, as she leapt on to Randall's back and pulled his crest, making him turn every colour imaginable. "She's not scared of you anymore, Randall! You're out of a job!" shouted Sulley.

Sulley grabbed Randall and threw him through an open door. Sulley and Mike dropped the door on to the Scare Floor, far below, where it shattered into tiny pieces. This meant that Randall would be stuck behind that door for a very long time!

Back on the Scare Floor, Sulley tricked Mr. Waternoose into following him into the simulator room and confessing everything, while Mike recorded it on tape. "Where will everyone get their screams now?" shouted Mr. Waternoose, as he was arrested by the CDA.

58

"Number one wants to talk to you," a CDA agent told Sulley. It was Roz! She had been working undercover for two years! Unfortunately, Sulley knew it was time to send Boo home.

"Someone bring me a door shredder," said Roz. "You mean, I can't see her again?" asked Sulley. "That's the way it has to be," replied Roz. Sulley gently carried Boo into her room and tucked her up in bed. "Goodbye, Boo. Kitty has to leave," said Sulley.

"Cheer up, pal. We got her home," said Mike, and he handed Sulley a piece of Boo's shredded door. "All right, we're both out of a job, but you know, we had some laughs along the way," added Mike. Suddenly, Sulley had a brilliant idea!

Continued on page 62...

THE LAUGH FLOOR

Business Shriek
www.businessshriek.com
A SLOBBER PRESS PUBLICATION
$1.682

MONSTERS, INC. BACK ON TOP!

James P. Sullivan, CEO

We are proud to announce that James P. Sullivan has put Monsters, Inc. back on top – where it belongs. More power is being produced than ever before by using the hilarious new technique of refining children's laughter.

NEW TECHNIQUES

Which technique has become the most successful at Monsters, Inc.?

Which technique is as successful as tripping over?

	Pie in the face	Tripping over	Making faces	Telling jokes	Making noises
30					
25					
20					
15					
10					
5					

JOLLY JUMBLE

Unscramble the letters to find four amusing words.

hlckeuc   **egilgg**

gahlu   **nufny**

MIKE'S METHOD

Mike Wazowski has some top tips to help you take up the laughter challenge. Follow his rules and you'll be laughing all the way.

a. **What makes you laugh?** Work this out and then do it.

b. **Laughter is contagious.** Find a friend who can make you laugh and then do the same for them, too.

c. **Make a laughter scrapbook.** Write down all the funny jokes you know and any funny things that have happened to you.

...Continued from page 59

Things had never been better at Monsters, Inc. The whole of Monstropolis was being powered by children's laughter rather than their screams. It was great fun working on the new Laugh Floor, but Sulley still missed his little Boo.

Mike knew how his best friend felt and arranged a surprise for him. "Sorry it took so long, pal, there was a lot of wood to go through," said Mike. Sulley lifted the final piece of Boo's door from his clipboard and put it in place.

The red light above the door lit up and Sulley excitedly opened the door.

"Boo!"

cried Sulley.

"Kitty!"

giggled Boo.

Why was the big, hairy, two-headed monster top of the class at school? Because two heads are better than one!

How do you greet a three-headed monster? Hello, hello, hello!

What happens if a big, hairy monster sits in front of you at the cinema? You miss most of the film!

What kind of monster can sit on the end of your finger? The bogeyman!

Did you hear about the ugly monster who sent his picture to a lonely hearts club? They sent it back saying they weren't that lonely!

What do monsters use to write with? Monsters Ink!

ANSWERS

THE SCARE FLOOR - 12/13

Pick a card Blue door - 64/36/7, yellow door - 6/14/45, green door - 12/4/21, purple door - 9/10/49.
Learn the routine 1, 4, 2, 6, 3, 5.
Scream control Two.

THE SCORE-BOARD - 14/15

Which Scarer? Jones.
Well done, Sulley

Scream total Sulley has collected the most screams after Door 4.
Door 3 - Sulley - 25, Randall - 26.
Door 4 - Sulley - 35, Randall - 34.

DECONTAMINATION - 24/25

Dial h-e-l-p 4, 3, 5, 7.
Child safety teddy bear
Contamination codes 9-17 - a child's slipper, 57-12 - a child's mobile, 43-12 - a child's ball, 4-13 - a child's doll.

THE SIMULATOR - 26/27

Practice makes perfect

BETTER HEALTH, BETTER STEALTH - 38/39

Give them a brush fang slime.

THE CANTEEN - 50/51

Today's lunch Snail slime, Toad warts, Bee stings.

PAPERWORK - 52/53

On time 1) Brown, Sam, 2) Li, Jay, 3) Gibbs, Mary, 4) Ray, Ian, 5) Richie, Jill.
In order Scare Floor B, Scare Floor F, Scare Floor J, Scare Floor S, Scare Floor U.
Fully corrected

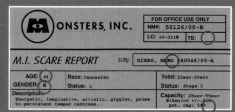

THE LAUGH FLOOR - 60/61

New techniques Pie in the face is the most successful technique. Telling jokes is as successful as tripping over.
Jolly jumble chuckle, giggle, laugh, funny.

More Disney fun in these super magazines!

Fab fun with all your Disney favourites!

Disney's Disney and Me

Puzzles
Stories
Fun things to
make and do!

On sale every
fortnight

FREE Sulley yo-yo key-ring!

Disney's Princess

You too can
be a Princess!

Posters
Stories
Crafts

On sale every four weeks

FREE Pretty Princess Pendant

Every girl can be a Princess!

Fun and games with Winnie and friends!

Disney's Winnie the Pooh

Stories
Colouring
Make-its

On sale every four weeks